# Spoilers

# Femdom Hypnosis and Mind Control Micro-Fiction

## S.B.

*The end is only the beginning.*

*Thank you to all patrons of Spell… B-O-U-N-D.*

# Table of Contents

# Introduction

Don't you hate it when you're invested in a book, a TV show or a movie and someone comes along and ruins all the surprises before you have the chance to say anything to the contrary? Well, in this case, you don't have to worry about spoilers because you already know how this goes. In this world of fetish and fantasy, all women make the rules, and all men obey them one way or another. Though you may believe otherwise, you are no exception.

Surrender your thoughts and your body to their irresistible charms in this new collection of mesmerizing micro-fiction. Do it now.

## No Place to Hide

Jason discovered the first camera by accident when a stray reflection hit his eyes. After that, unearthing the other devices proved to be a cinch. That had to be the work of his crazy ex-girlfriend Daisy, but why?

When all twelve flashed simultaneously enveloping his mind in a blinding, hypnotic light, the truth became clear.

## Tender and Sweet

"Love me tender, love me sweet…"

Charles did. He loved his enchantress.

"Never let me go…"

Of course not! Preposterous!

"You have made my life complete

And I love you so."

So true, He loved to hear her sing and lose his mind.

Too bad he realized far too late she was also a cannibal.

# Mindfuck

"What's up, Tim?"

"I think I've been mindfucked, John."

"By whom?"

"I don't know."

"When?"

"I don't know."

"How?"

"I don't know, okay?"

"If you don't know anything, how do you know you've been mindfucked?"

"Well…"

"You weren't."

"Huh?"

"You were never mindfucked."

"Never?"

"Never. You're just imagining things. Now thank me."

"Thank you, Johanna."

## Tracking Beacon

Cameron's doppelgänger stared at him.

"Greetings. I've come from your future. In 2029, a group of female warrior aliens will find this planet through a modified tracking beacon and brainwash thousands of men. You will be the first to succumb."

"So… is this a warning?" Present day Cameron asked.

"No. I just planted the beacon."

## Nothing at All

Cole shook his head. He was forgetting something but what? Perhaps his girlfriend knew.

"Mara? What happened today? I'm… confused."

"Nothing important happened today," she cooed. "Nothing at all."

"Okay then," he sighed, conditioning taking over.

As he left the room, she glanced at the jar atop the fireplace. He didn't need his balls anyway.

# Hypnotic Checkmate

Stella had said: "the secret to win at chess is to plan ahead."

However, she had also said: "If you don't checkmate me in ten moves, I'll turn you into my mindless plaything."

"Oh fuck!" Gary thought. "Not like this. Nine moves… no, eight… fuck, fuck, fuck!"

Stella smiled happily, knowing she had already won.

## Special Promotion

The sign read:

"Ladies, spend five hundred dollars and take home a hypnotized man-servant for free!"

"Excuse me?" Darren blurted.

"Don't like our promotion, sir?" the store clerk asked.

"No. This is outrageous!"

"Our stock of slaves disagrees."

"And how have you amassed a stock of slaves?"

"From all the men that complain…" she grinned.

## She Happened

"You're all sweaty. What happened?" Frank asked.

"She did," Alex replied.

"What did she do?"

"She said I was becoming a lazy bastard so she mindfucked me."

"How?"

"Not sure, but now every time I hear her name, I have to jog five miles."

"I can't believe Paula did that."

"Fuck!" Alex started to run.

## The Rain Must Fall

"It's inevitable. Your surrender has always been inevitable. Now that your mind is wide open. It's time for your will to crumble, and mine take over. The rain must fall and so must you," Julie cooed. "Obey."

"Yes, Princess," Brandon replied, the only two words she would allow him to remember when he woke up.

## The Man in the Iron Cage

The prisoner's identity was finally revealed.

"It's the King!" Porthos said.

"Try brainwashed slave," Milady de Winter chuckled.

"What did you do?" D'Artagnan asked.

"See for yourself," she undid his robe, revealing the metal cage.

"Gross!" Aramis and Athos screamed.

"Plenty to go around. All for one and one for all, right?"

The Musketeers fled.

## Hypnotist's Clothes

"Oh no!" Gavin muttered, shaking his head.

"What's wrong?" Corinne asked.

"You're wearing your hypnotist's clothes again!"

"Am I?" She smirked.

"Yes. That dress… that belt… those boots… whenever you put them on, I know I'm going to be mindfucked."

"Perhaps you already are."

"Huh?"

"Touch, big boy."

His trembling hands cupped her naked breasts.

## No Parking

The policewoman tapped on the driver's window.

"Yes, Officer?" Conrad asked.

"This is a no parking zone. You either pay a fine right now or…"

"Yes?"

"… you let me mindfuck you because I'm horny."

"Ah," he grabbed his phone.

"What are you doing?"

"Calling my boss to let him know I'll be late for work."

## Deamonica

Once hidden by glamour, the velvet red horns were now visible in-between her wavy hair.

"Demon!" Jay spat.

"Goddess…" Monica smiled.

"Whatever… I will never worship you, foul creature!"

"Right…" Her dark tail swung from side to side, first capturing his eyes and then his mind. "You were saying?"

"May I please lick your pussy?"

## Lucky Bastard

"Alan?" His father said. "I thought you were dead!"

"I've never been more alive," he replied.

"What happened?"

"After the crash, a woman nursed me back to health. Then, she brainwashed me and turned into her slave. Now, if you'll excuse me, I need to go drain my bank account."

"Lucky bastard…" his father mumbled.

## All Yours

Jenna sat on the couch, legs wide open.

"You need this, don't you, boy?"

"Y-yes," Frank stammered.

"Beg then."

"Please, Mistress. I need it! Please let me have it!"

"All yours," she threw him the apron she'd been hiding under her ass much to his confusion.

"You win again," he conceded.

Domme 327, slave 0.

## Please Click…

The image CAPTCHA on Eliza's website was quite something.

"Click on all spirals until there are none," it said.

Harold hit the first, black and blue flashing. He hit the second, pink emerging from yellow. He hit the third, envious green and lustrous red.

After the two hundredth and fifty-second, his mind was completely blank.

## Wonderful

It was Tuesday, time for the customary routine.

Jacob entered Lara's bedroom, sat on the metallic chair in the corner and watched as she removed his positronic brain for upgrades and a bit of polish.

"Wonderful," he muttered before the OS shut down entirely.

Life was so much better ever since he had been robotized.

# June's Birthday

Alicia's dress was stunning.

"Where are you going all dressed up?" Timothy asked.

"June's birthday party."

"Right… bought her a present yet?"

"I have you…"

"You're sharing me? We agreed not do that."

"You agreed, not me and since you can't resist my conditioning…"

She snapped her fingers and the human present crawled behind her.

## Renovations

"Honey, when you talked about renovations…" Jack mumbled.

"Yes?" Trish grinned, make-up kit in hand.

"I thought you wanted me to paint the kitchen, not this!"

"Oh, you'll still do it but as my sissy maid."

"No! I'll fight it!"

"Liar…" she applied blush on his left cheek, the feathery touch immediately triggering an erection.

# Normal Pets

"This is my sweet tarantula," Amber said.

"Ewww," Denise shivered.

"And this is my beautiful python."

"Disgusting! Damn, girl! Why can't you have normal pets like everyone else?"

"Normal, huh?"

"Yeah."

"This way, please."

They stopped in front of a mirror and then Amber muttered: "This is my hypnotized slut."

Denise blushed and sank deeper.

## Coffee Break

Samantha loved her coffee with a dash of Ceylon Cinnamon.

Anne could never say 'no' to coconut milk ice cubes on hers.

For Rebecca, black was always the way to go.

Their best friend Greg liked his with tonic and enough mind control drugs to wipe his persona clean… but he didn't know it yet.

## Too Hot

"Why is it so hot?" Bernard queried, glazed eyes.

"I think it's the boxers," Jaime suggested. "You should lose them."

"But then I'll be naked!"

"So? No time for modesty. It's too hot. You must strip."

"Yes, I must."

The other ten women in the room laughed as he remained blissfully unaware of their presence.

## Brick Wall

"Corinne? Why are you mad? So, what if Jill tranced me? You said it was okay! Corinne? Damn, sometimes talking to you is like talking to a brick wall!"

Suddenly, Walter blinked, trance dissipating. He found himself outside the house, staring at the following message:

"I am a brick wall."

Her humor was something else.

## Never Be a Dick

"Come on, stop laughing!" Horace begged.

"I can't…" Ralph confessed.

"You really think it's funny?"

"A ten-hour long erection? Yeah, I do. No Viagra, huh?"

"No, just hypnosis."

"I see Amanda knows her stuff. Remind me to never be a dick to her."

"You said that on purpose, didn't you?"

"Yeah…" Ralph kept on laughing.

## The Invention

Clara's new invention was a technological marvel: a self-contained VR cubicle where one could create and train a slave in all things kinky and bizarre.

Eager to unleash her dominant side, Bonnie gave the machine a test run and when the lights went down, the fun began.

She realized too late the slave was her.

## Not Today

Viktor lay suspended, bound by thick rope when Mistress Julia walked in.

"Happy I'm back, slave?" She asked.

"Mmmmmm…" he mumbled.

"What's that? Cat got your tongue?"

"Mmmmmm…"

"No, not a cat but a hypnotist…" she fetched a whip.

"Mmmmmm…"

"You know why I did it, right? You scream a lot…."

"Mmmmmm…"

"… but not today…"

## A Good Man

"Denise, am I a good man?" Charles asked.

"Of course not," she replied, not even looking at him.

"Huh? I'm not?"

"No. You're a a good puppy, a good maid, and a good slave especially when you're under. Being a man has nothing to do with it."

"Meaning…?"

"You're going to love the name Charlene."

## Cumming on Command

Joel's cock followed the movements of Helen's right index finger, going up and down.

"How are you doing this?" he queried.

"Hypnotic suggestion," she replied before simulating a sharp pinch. The sudden pain almost made him explode.

"I'm not cumming on command…"

"Give me five minutes…" she smiled.

He was licking every drop after two.

# Newbie

"Let me guess, first time?" Princess Angie asked.

"That obvious?" Nicholas replied.

"Yes. Don't worry, I love hypno-newbies."

"That's good. So… how will I know?"

"Know what?"

"If I'm hypnotized or not."

"You won't because if you do then I'm doing it wrong, however…"

"Yes?"

"I never do it wrong."

Nicholas smiled and went deeper.

## Cute

"Hmm… Jane?"

"What is it, Sophie?"

"What's wrong with your husband? He's at the driveway, on all fours, barking at the cars."

"He said he envied dog's life, so I hypnotized him into believing he's one. Doesn't he look cute, wagging his tail?"

"No! He just tried to bite me!"

"Yeah, my dog hates pussies…"

# Prescription

"Hello, Dr. Evans."

"Hello, Bill."

"You said these pills would help me regain my memories…"

"I did. Has something started coming back to you?"

"I think so. Have I always been your slave?"

"Yes, Bill. So glad you finally remembered. Let me up your prescription for faster results."

"Okay, Dr…. and thank you."

"You're welcome."

## A Study

Andy picked up his cell.

"Hello?"

"Good afternoon. My name is Natasha from HypnoInc. We're conducting a study on suggestibility. Can you go into trance for me right now?"

"I suppose…"

"Perfect. Just listen to my voice…"

He hung up ten hours later, no clothes, no house, and no money left on his bank account.

## Emergency Call

"911, what's your emergency?"

"Please help me!" A man cried out. "She's trying to brainwash me, turn me into her… Oh God, she's coming, she… AHHHHH!"

"Sir? Sir, are you there?"

"Please forgive my husband," a cold woman's voice was heard. "He suffers from delusions and forgot to take his pills."

The call went dead.

## She was Tired

"Well?" Lance asked the moment Jonah walked in the office.

"Well, what?"

"How many times did Becca hypnotize you last weekend? 'cause I made a pool, you know?"

"You're betting on my trances now?"

"It's fun. I chose five. It was five, right?"

"Nope."

"How many then?"

"Just thirty-one… she was tired."

Lance's jaw dropped.

## Left Alone

Sean and Clark stormed the house.

"Where's your brother?" their father asked.

"He…"

"Spill it, Clark!"

"Brooke Manor. The witch controls his mind now."

"And you left him alone? Why?!!!"

"Because this dumbass resisted her charms and dragged me with him!" Sean sighed. "Sorry, I have to go."

He ran back out, eager for oblivion.

## Blood Sings

The light of the rotating blades reflected on Derrick's half-open eyes.

"I… I don't think I want to do this…" he muttered as they drew closer.

"Thoughts are irrelevant…" Martina coaxed him. "Sacrifice is mandatory."

"But…"

"Shhh… Obey. Forget. Tonight, blood sings!"

Derrick's mind disappeared forever the moment his cock and balls were torn apart.

## I Tell You Many Things…

"It's finally October…" Cordelia mused.

"So?" Harold asked.

"My birthday is in October."

"You said January last time. And June before that. And…"

"Stop!" she interrupted him. "I tell you many things while you're under. You're the one that believes everything."

"Not true."

"My birthday is today…"

"Fuck!" He rushed to buy her a present.

# Civic Duty

"May I help you?" the latex-clad guard asked.

"I found this male in an alley…" Nadine pointed at a naked man.

"I see. Serial number?"

"Unknown. It was scrapped. It appears self-inflicted."

"Failed brainwashing, most likely. Thank you for bringing this to my attention."

"Just fulfilling my civic duty…" Nadine smiled before heading her way.

## Basic Math

"Let's try this again," Emily said. "How much is six times three?"

"Zero," Patrick replied.

"Five minus two?" She laughed.

"Zero."

"Eight plus six?"

"Zero."

"Oh my, you must be really in a trance if you've forgotten how to do basic math. What's on your mind?"

"Zero will, zero worries, zero resistance," he drooled.

"Bingo!"

## Distracting

"As you can see, our profits are… Hmmm, Mr. Reynolds, are you even listening to me?" Chloe frowned.

"Sorry…" he mumbled. "That spiral chart is so distracting."

"How distracting?"

"Well…" His cock sprang to attention.

"Excellent!" She grinned.

Chloe got a raise, a new car, and an obedient slave before the end of the meeting.

## Really?

"Really?"

"Yes. Really."

"But…"

"But what?"

"I thought…"

"I know. You always do that."

"Not always."

"You're doing it now."

"No, I'm not!"

"So, you're not thinking?"

"No."

"Just listening to my voice?"

"Yes."

"And enjoying it?"

"Yes."

"Want to listen more and more, drop more and more?"

"Yes, please."

"Really?

"Yes. Really."

"Good pet."

**The Switch**

"You're a switch?" Dennis asked. "How does it feel?"

"You got it wrong," Gene replied. "I'm not a switch, I have a switch."

"Switch for what?"

"Allow me to demonstrate," Gene's girlfriend smiled and touched the back of his neck.

"Gina mode activated," he droned before leaving the room to try out a new dress.

## Perfect

"Fuck!" Victor growled.

"What's wrong?" Gemma asked.

"I can't finish this stanza."

"Let me hear it."

"Okay," he began:

"I am the voice in every season's call,

I am the hope your soul wishes to be

And when the trees fell into Fall…"

"… Your mind forever fell into Me." She concluded.

"Perfect…" he sighed, dreamily.

## New Model

"It's fried?" Karen asked.

"Yes, Miss. This chip is gone." The technician replied.

"Well… replace it then!"

"Here's the problem: The Obedient Husband line has been discontinued a long time ago. Nowadays, I only carry the new model in stock."

"Which is…?"

"Obedient Sissy Husband."

"Sorry, Alec," Karen thought as she pulled her credit card.

## All in His Head

"Do something!" Bonnie cried out. "He's burning up."

"We can't;" Doctor Waters replied.

"Why not?"

"Because this is all in his head and he's not snapping out of it. Where's the hypnotist that planted the suggestion?"

"I don't know. She took all his money and bailed."

"Well, unless you find her…"

Brett languished in pain.

## Skipping Numbers

"Can you count backwards from ten for me?" Mischa asked.

"Sure," Sergei replied, half-dazed. "Ten, nine, eight, six, four…"

"You're skipping numbers, sweetie."

"I am?"

"Yes. And skipping thoughts, too."

"Oh. I am sorry, Mis…"

"Mistress," she completed. "Or did you forget?"

"I guess…" he blinked.

"Don't do it again," she cooed.

He never did.

**Safety Off**

Melanie put Paul under and brought him back up again. It was the tenth time in a row.

"Stop!" He begged.

"Huh?"

"Stop!"

"What's the safeword?"

"I don't know, you made me forget!"

"Too bad." She grinned.

Melanie put Paul under and brought him back up again. It was the fiftieth time in a row.

## Easy Freshmen

"Are you seeing this?" Dennis asked, eyes glued to the microscope.

"Yeah," Mark agreed. "These cells look like spirals."

"They're so pretty. I could sit here looking at them all day."

"So could I. Can we?" He begged.

"Please do," Miss Morrow, their Biology teacher said. She loved easy freshmen first thing in the morning.

## Buyer's Remorse

George looked at the expensive items laid on his bed and mumbled:

"A leather dress, designer thigh-high boots, a diamond choker… Why did I buy all this?"

"Because you're an obedient hypnoslave, hubby," Wanda replied.

"You did this?"

"Yes, but the fun starts now."

"Meaning…?"

"Time to pimp you out. sissy," she snapped her fingers.

# Gone Missing

Male, forty-two, goes by "Bob". Last seen on Main Street wearing a red shirt and blue jeans while screaming: "Freedom at last!". Very docile except when he gets confused. His trigger is "Bitch Doll". If you see him, please call 500-MUSTOBEY. His owner is worried sick she won't get to complete his reprogramming. Thank you.

## Universal Shadow

Jim examined another body.

"This one is empty, too," he said.

"Fuck!" Devon shouted. "What could have erased their minds like this?"

"Goddess…" the ship's captain mumbled, eyes going blank. "I'm sorry, but you need to understand she's more powerful than anything we've ever encountered."

The alien shadow crept inside the bridge, all hope lost.

## Is it Done?

"Is it done?" Aaron asked.

"Yes, the triggers are set," Juliette replied.

"I don't feel different. How will I know?"

"Trust me. When I take control, you will know."

"Side effects?"

"Some people experience amnesia right after, but it's rare."

"Okay."

There was silence for a few minutes and then Aaron asked:

"Is it done?"

## Blank Space

"… and this is us by the Niagara Falls," Judy said.

"During our honeymoon?" Patrick mumbled.

"Yes. So glad you're starting to remember our life together."

"Not sure how I ever forgot…"

"That's okay, you're forgiven…" She touched his forehead. "Deeper now."

"Yes, Judy."

She grabbed another piece of paper and continued filling in the blanks.

## The Heart Knows

Compelled beyond reason, Trevor knocked on Greta's door. When she opened it, he knelt silently.

Looking down, she saw the scar on his chest and asked:

"You're the one that received Jonathan's heart, aren't you?"

"Yes," he mumbled.

"He was my slave, and now so are you. Come."

He crawled behind her, mind in chains.

## Spoilers

"Reading my book?" Cliff asked.

"Skimming. I know how it ends." Martha replied.

" Really? Do tell."

"She's going to hypnotize him in the last page and turn him into her slave, duh!"

"Not true, sorry."

"Sooner then?"

"Page 293." He blushed.

"Ah, this one…"

She laid down the book as he fell to his knees.

# Conclusion

What did I tell you? There was never any doubt that you were destined to lose your mind. You loved it, and now you want more, don't you? In that case, please visit my personal website - https://www.sbspellbound.net – and discover all the fantasies of the mind waiting for you there. Also, please consider supporting my efforts if you want to see more of them in the future. Thank you in advance and have fun.